JAKE
IN SPACE
SAVING SATURN

Candice Lemon-Scott
Illustrated by Celeste Hulme

'Come here ... come here and ... *gotcha!*'

Jake caught a floating red space jube in his mouth and munched it noisily, then sat back in his seat. He and his friends – Skye, Milly, Rory and Henry – were having the best time on their mystery flight. The flight was their reward from the Central Intergalactic Agency (CIA) for solving their last mission. Even now Jake could hardly believe that they had helped stop all the planets in the solar system from being destroyed.

He looked around the cabin of the Galactic Explorer 5000. It was so wide Jake and his friends sat next to each other in one long row. In front of him there was a screen. He reached up and switched it on. A holographic film began to play. Even though he knew it wasn't real, Jake found himself closing his eyes when a space racer came shooting forward as though it was going to hit him.

He switched the movie off after a while and sat back up. A hover tray, covered by a clear dome, brought over floating space snacks. Jake lifted the dome, squeezed his hand under and grabbed hold of a floating ooze cake. He nearly choked as he bit into it and a shot of thick chocolate squirted down his throat. Rory laughed at Jake and grabbed a cake for himself, accidentally squirting chocolate in his eye.

 2

'Oooh!' Milly squealed. 'I wonder what this button does.'

She pressed a silver button on the side of her chair. It reclined back into a bed and the headrest puffed up into a soft pillow.

'Wow!' Jake said.

'I wonder where we're going,' Skye said, squinting at the galactic map on her screen. Henry was silently staring at his map too.

Jake didn't mind at all that he had no idea where they were going. That was half the fun of it. He didn't even have to navigate. The mystery flight was running on automatic pilot and he was enjoying every minute of it. He wasn't trying to get his space car licence or stop missiles from destroying a planet. Here he could daydream as much as he liked and no-one minded at all.

He pressed the button on the side of his chair and felt it fill with air until it was softer than his real bed at home. He closed his eyes. He imagined himself floating among the stars, cartwheeling and somersaulting …

Then there was a quick tap on his shoulder. It was Skye, trying to get his attention.

'Enough with the space snoring! Look at your screen,' she said.

Jake switched his screen back on but this time he set it to projection. Saturn shone out in front of their car, its rings clearer than he had ever seen before.

'Saturn!' Jake gasped. Milly and Rory switched on their screens too. They had all flown around Saturn before, in the Rocket Battles space car race, but they had never seen it like this.

'What do we do now?' asked Jake.

'*Do?*' Skye replied. She looked at him, then leaned over and grabbed a jar from Henry's

4

seat tray. 'I think you should do something with your hair first,' she laughed. It was Henry's no-gravity hair wax.

'Do not use too much of that,' said Henry. He turned to look at Jake and his eyes widened. 'However, *you* may require more than is usual.'

Rory snorted with laughter. *Oh no*, Jake thought. *Is it really that bad?* He felt on top of his head. His hair had blown up into its usual frizzball in zero gravity. He pulled out a small glob of the wax and sniffed it. At least it smelled all right now. The last lot had been disgusting. He pressed his hair down flat and handed the jar back to Henry.

'Much better,' Skye said, smiling.

Jake grinned then turned to his screen. 'So, is that where the mystery flight is taking us?'

'It appears so,' said Henry, staring hard at his screen.

'Saturn?' Rory piped up. 'It's a gas planet.

How would we land this car on it? It has a heap of fast-flying asteroids around its middle. We can't be going there.'

'Well, it looks like we're heading straight for it,' said Milly nervously.

Jake looked at his screen again. They were getting closer to the ringed planet. Icy chunks of space dust spun around at super-fast speed.

'We're on automatic pilot,' said Skye. 'We can't exactly steer away from the rings, or avoid the asteroids.'

'So, what's your advice, Mr I-Know-Everything?' Rory said, raising his eyebrows in Henry's direction as if it was all Henry's fault.

'I am certain we are perfectly safe,' Henry replied, ignoring Rory's rudeness. 'We are on a mystery flight, not a mission.'

Jake laughed, nearly choking on a jube.

At that moment, the car leaned a little to

the right. If Jake hadn't been buckled in he would have slid straight into Skye. The space car shifted upwards, moving above the rings.

'See?' Henry said, casually catching a jube in his mouth and swallowing. 'It is just as I expected. The craft is well-programmed. Now I shall take a rest.'

With that, Henry shut himself down.

'Brilliant,' grumbled Rory. 'We're trying not to get hit by flying rocks but our CIA cyborg needs his beauty sleep.'

'The Galactic Explorer 5000 knows what it's doing, Rory,' Skye said. 'And Henry's not much fun when he's low on battery power, remember?'

'I know,' sighed Rory and he vacuumed a yellow jube into his mouth.

Jake stared at his screen again. Could they really be headed to Saturn? What would they do there? He knew there were people on Saturn but they all lived on a megaship. If it was anything like the drab grey research stations he'd seen, he couldn't imagine it would be much fun. Suddenly the mystery flight didn't seem so exciting after all.

The Galactic Explorer 5000 flew above Saturn's rings and over the top of the planet. Then it began dropping down to the other side of Saturn and Jake nearly leaped out of his seat in amazement when he looked closely at his projection screen.

'Wow!' he exclaimed. 'You have to take a look at this.'

The others looked up at their screens. Milly squealed excitedly. Skye laughed and clapped her hands and Rory looked like he'd just seen a space bug doing cartwheels through a burning hoop. As if he had heard them, Henry switched himself back on and looked too.

There in front of them, on the other side of Saturn, was the megaship. But it wasn't an ordinary megaship. This one gleamed brighter than a star, blazing gold like the Sun in Earth's sky. Along the sides it glittered with gems, from the deepest blue sapphire to the brightest red ruby. A strip of glowing crystals marked out a runway on the ship's surface. Jake let out a huge breath, only just realising he'd been holding it in.

'I didn't know the people of Saturn had a place like *this* to live!' Jake said.

'Yeah, I want to live there too,' Rory laughed.

'It's fantastic!' Milly cried.

'This is going to be better than the Floating Hotel of Venus,' Skye agreed.

Jake thought back to the incredible food and games of the hotel. It looked like they were in for a whole lot of fun here too. If this was just the outside, what would the ship look like on the inside? He was so excited it took him a moment to notice Henry. He was standing at the control panel, madly pressing buttons.

'What are you doing, Henry?' Jake asked him.

'The automatic pilot has been overridden,' Henry said. 'We're off-course.'

'He really doesn't know how to have fun,' Rory sighed.

'That is not a megaship. That is a *pirate* ship!' Henry cried, still pressing buttons. 'They have reprogrammed the autopilot.'

'Is your head full of space dust?' Jake laughed. 'Of course it's not a pirate ship.'

'Yes, it is. I have seen photographs of them and they look just like this,' Henry said.

'In old storybooks maybe. There's no such thing as pirates,' Rory scoffed.

'The CIA has it wrong. We're supposed to be saving Saturn,' Henry said. He had opened the panel in his arm and was pulling out tools, trying to fit them into the control panel.

'Ha! So we *are* on another mission?' Jake said.

'I should have known!' snorted Rory, but Henry clamped his mouth shut.

'I think you'd better sit down, Henry,' Skye said softly. 'It looks like we're coming in to land.'

Skye was right. They'd reached the landing strip on top of the megaship. The Galactic Explorer 5000 slid smoothly across the glassy surface then came to a stop. Moments later the car tilted forward. The ground beneath them had opened up, like a trapdoor, and the Explorer slid down into the megaship. The trapdoor closed above them.

Jake looked at Henry. The cyborg was still pressing buttons even though they'd landed. 'Come on Henry,' Jake sighed. 'No-one's seen a pirate in thousands of years.'

'This is not the mission!' repeated Henry. 'I am not stepping out of this car.'

'Well I'm sick of missions,' said Rory. 'Let's see what this ship is like inside.'

They undid their seatbelts and Jake opened the hatch.

Looking around, Jake saw that they had landed inside a huge hangar. It was dazzling. The walls shone with gold, and a large doorway opposite them was lined with precious stones. 'Whoa,' whispered Skye.

Rory's eyes lit up. 'And this is just the car park!'

'I'll get Henry,' Jake said, but at that moment,

the door of the hangar slid open. Four people entered the room – two men and two women. They were dressed in the finest silk robes of deep purple, emerald green, bright red and indigo blue, and wore jewelled crowns on their heads. Their slippers were so soft that their footsteps could hardly be heard as they moved across the room towards them. Jake didn't know if they were royalty but they sure looked like it.

'Welcome!' the woman in purple said, smiling. 'I am Violet, captain of the Saturn megaship.'

The woman in red said, 'I am Ruby.' She pointed to the two men. 'This is Indigo and Em.'

Jake saw Milly and Skye curtsy, so he dipped his head in a slight bow. Rory was standing with his mouth hanging open like he was waiting to catch a floating jube. Jake nudged him and he made an awkward bow too. The four people stood staring at them as though waiting for them to say something. Jake frowned, unsure what was expected of them.

'And you are?' Violet said.

'Er ... sorry,' Jake stammered. 'I thought you would have known our names from the mystery flight guest list?'

Violet let out a tinkling laugh, 'Oh yes, of course, but we don't know which of you is which on your, ah ...'

'Mystery flight?' Skye filled in.

'Yes, of course, the mystery flight,' Violet replied, smiling tightly.

Jake introduced himself and his friends and Violet seemed to relax after that.

'Have you heard about our megaship before?' Violet said.

Jake was so in awe he could only shake his

head. He was pulled out of his trance when he heard thundering footsteps vibrating in the floor beneath him. The sound was coming from behind and he turned. Henry had leaped out of the car and was running towards them, waving a jack like it was a sword. He looked like he was going into battle.

'Pirates!' Henry screamed as he ran across the hangar.

The four robed people laughed. The sound was so soft and musical it was like the tinkling of jewels. *Pirates?* There was no way these peaceful people could be pirates!

'Henry! Stop!' Skye said.

Violet and the others didn't seem at all worried. They stood calmly and watched Henry running towards them.

But Jake knew how strong Henry was. He could actually hurt someone. As the cyborg raced past Jake, not even seeming to notice him, Jake leaped at him and grabbed his arm. Rory skidded over to help hold Henry while Jake pulled open the skin on Henry's arm and pressed a button. Henry was shut down straightaway.

'Ah, sorry about that,' Jake said, trying to force a smile. 'Must have a bad connection somewhere.'

'It would seem so,' Indigo agreed thoughtfully.

'Never mind,' Violet said. 'I'm sure he can be repaired later. But now that you are our special mystery flight guests, I suppose you would like it if we showed you around?'

Jake and his friends left Henry in the hangar. Jake felt bad about shutting Henry down, but quickly forgot about it as they were led into a glittering golden hallway.

'You don't think it's real gold, do you?' Skye whispered to Jake.

'Everything you see here is genuine,' Violet said.

Jake was surprised she had been able to

18

hear what Skye had said. He looked over at Skye and saw that she was blushing a deeper red than Ruby's robes.

'Are you ... are you royalty?' Milly asked quietly.

Violet laughed her tinkling laugh. 'Oh, not quite.'

She continued to float down the hallway and they all followed. Jake looked around at the gleaming walls. They were amazing, but something felt strange. If the entire population of Saturn lived here, where were the people? He couldn't see or hear anyone else. He thought back to Henry running and yelling out that Violet and her friends were pirates. That couldn't be true!

'Ah, here we are,' said Violet, stopping at a huge set of crystal doors. Indigo stepped forward and pushed them open.

Jake walked through the doorway and all

thoughts of pirates disappeared. The room was exactly how he imagined a royal hall would look. On one side was a long table with rows of high-backed wooden chairs. They were decorated with animal carvings and gemstones, and had red velvet seats. Silver goblets and cutlery were set at each place. On the other side of the room was a shiny black ballroom floor. Jake stepped over to it. When he looked down he could see his face reflected back at him. He recognised this – the floor was made of obsidian, the same shiny rock that the evil Valerie had used to build her castle on Venus. He looked up. Crystal chandeliers hung from the ceiling, reflecting rainbows of light around the room.

'What do you think?' Violet asked.

'It's the most beautiful place I've ever seen,' Milly gasped.

Violet's laugh echoed around the room,

20

sounding like a thousand bells chiming at once.

'Hungry?' Ruby asked.

'Oh yes,' Skye and Milly said together.

Ruby clapped her hands and a procession of people carrying large silver platters entered the room. They had their heads bowed as they laid the steaming plates on the table.

'Mmmm!' Rory exclaimed. 'This beats space snacks any day!'

Jake felt a bit squirmy – servants were something he had only read about in books. Now robots did all the serving jobs that people once did. He caught the eye of one of the servants but the man quickly looked away again. When all the plates were laid the servants moved back out through the doors.

'Please! Sit,' Violet said.

Jake pulled back a heavy chair and sat down at the long table. Milly, Skye and Rory did the same. Even with the four of them and their four hosts, the huge room looked strangely empty with so many chairs at the table.

'We shall leave you to enjoy your supper,' Violet said.

Indigo placed a small silver bell down in the centre of the table. 'If you need anything, just ring.'

They slid quietly out of the room and the four friends were left alone.

Rory, Milly and Skye quickly began filling their plates with food and poured drinks into the silver goblets. Jake couldn't bring himself to eat though.

'Jake?' Skye said, noticing. 'What's the matter?'

'I don't know,' Jake said. 'Something just doesn't feel right.'

'What do you mean?' Milly asked. 'This is a

pretty amazing mystery flight location, don't you think?'

'I guess. But where are all the people?' he whispered.

'It's a big ship,' Skye said.

'Why didn't Violet seem to have a clue what I was talking about when I mentioned the mystery flight?'

'You're sounding just like Henry,' Rory muttered, gulping down food. 'Relax and just enjoy it. We can live like kings, even if it's only for a day.'

Jake shrugged and filled his plate. 'I guess I'm thinking about Henry,' he said. 'But maybe Rory was right. The megaship was so huge that all the people were probably just in a different part of it. He decided to ask Violet when she came back in.

'Speaking of Henry,' Skye said, 'we'd better go wake him up after this.'

'Oh yes,' Milly said between mouthfuls, 'poor Henry. I'm sure he'll be okay though.'

Jake filled his plate until he started to feel a bit sick from all the rich and sweet food he'd scoffed down. He washed it down with a big goblet of dew juice. When they were finished eating, soft music began to play. It was as though the room knew they had finished. Jake noticed the girls had started to tap their feet to the music. Skye nudged him gently.

'Do you, ah, want to dance?' she asked, gesturing to the dance floor.

Jake nearly spat out his last sip of juice. *Me? Dance?* he thought. *No way!* He frowned and shook his head. 'No thanks,' he replied politely.

'Come on, it'll be fun.'

Jake looked over at Rory, who had started choking on a space cake at the idea of dancing.

But surprisingly Rory let Milly take his hand and lead him onto the obsidian floor. Then Jake knew he would have to go along with it too.

The moment he stepped awkwardly onto the dance floor, Jake felt embarrassed. He really had no idea how to dance. He had made sure he skipped all the dance lessons at school and now he just wished he could disappear. Skye held one of his hands and placed the other on his shoulder.

'Just step forward, to the side and then together,' she said. 'That's all there is to it.'

What was it she just said? Was it sideways first or forward?

But before Jake knew it he was actually moving and not standing on Skye's toes. He started to think he was better at this dancing business than he'd thought. Then he felt a light rush of air beneath his feet and he realised it was the floor. The air flowing from it had lifted them and they were actually floating above the surface. They were flying!

'This … this isn't too bad,' Jake said.

'As long as none of my friends on Mars ever find out about it,' Rory said.

Jake turned to see Rory flip in the air and then spin above the ground on his back like an upside-down space bug.

It seemed like just moments before the music ended and the air flow stopped. Jake's feet returned to the polished black floor. Rory fell on his back on the hard ground.

'Ouch!' Rory moaned, rubbing his back as he pulled himself up. Skye smiled and dropped her hands.

'We've been here a while. Let's go get Henry,' she said.

'Should we call Violet first?' Jake suggested, looking at the bell.

'No, I remember the way,' Skye replied. 'We can bring him straight back here.'

The huge crystal doors were shimmering on the far side of the room. Jake walked across to them and gave the doors a push but they wouldn't open. Skye, Milly and Rory came up behind him.

'What is it, Jake?' asked Skye.

Jake felt the dew juice swirl like a whirlpool in his stomach as fear gripped him.

'We're locked in.'

'Why have they locked the doors?' Milly asked, looking uneasy.

'So we don't steal all their fancy jewels, I suppose,' Rory said, but he didn't look so sure.

'Maybe,' Skye said. 'Looks like we'll have to ring for them now though.'

She walked over to the table and jingled the small silver bell. Despite its size it made a loud chiming sound that echoed around the room.

Seconds later the doors opened and Violet appeared, followed by Ruby, Indigo and Em.

'How was your meal?' Violet asked smoothly.

'Wonderful!' Milly answered.

'Good,' she said. 'Now, it is getting late. You will stay here the night?'

'Isn't that what you do on a mystery flight?' Skye asked. 'Stay over?'

'Of course, of course. It's just, ah, some only come for a very short visit,' Violet said shakily. 'I'll show you to your rooms for the night.' The four turned around so Jake and his friends could follow.

'Wait!' Jake said.

Violet spun around soundlessly. Jake thought he saw a dark scowl on her face but the next moment she was smiling calmly and he was sure he must have just imagined it.

'Yes?' she drawled.

'Um, it's our friend Henry,' Jake said nervously. 'Can we please go and get him first?'

Violet lifted her index finger and signalled for him to wait. She turned around to Ruby and the two men. They bent their heads together and whispered among themselves. Then Violet turned back around.

'We have decided it would be best if we got him for you,' Violet said.

'But ...'

Violet put her hand up to silence Jake. 'You must be tired and need your rest. He is a cyborg, correct?'

Jake nodded.

'Then we are well-equipped to reactivate him,' Violet said. 'Our helpers will take you to your rooms and Henry will join you presently.'

Before Jake could protest, the four floated away. He hadn't even had a chance to ask about all the other people on the ship. As they passed two servants Violet whispered something to one of them.

When the two servants reached them they didn't speak but gestured for Jake and his friends to follow them, their heads still bent so low that Jake couldn't even look them in the eye. They walked back up the golden hall but this time took a turn to the right, midway along.

Jake and his friends talked quietly. Skye teased Jake about how easily he danced in the end.

'Yeah, I didn't stand on your feet, but that was only because I was floating at the time,' Jake said, grinning in embarrassment.

He looked up and saw one of the servants staring at him. He gave Jake a sharp but knowing look, as though he had something important to say but he quickly dipped his head before Jake could speak. This time Jake had an even stronger feeling that the man wanted to tell him something. He decided he would ask the others about it later, when they were alone again.

The hall they were walking down seemed to go on forever, but after a few minutes they reached another set of doors. One of the servants pushed them open.

'This … this is our room?' Milly sputtered.

The servant nodded. Jake looked around in awe. This wasn't just a room. It was like a small house. Rory raced in, jumping straight onto a huge king-size four-poster bed. He stretched out on it like a starfish and laughed.

One of the servants cleared his throat. 'This is the girls' dormitory. If you'll follow us, your room is next door.'

Rory rolled off the bed, embarrassed. 'Oh,

ah … yeah, I knew that.'

The girls laughed and waved goodbye to Jake and Rory. The two boys followed the servants to the next room. This was just as huge as the girls' room but it was decorated in darker colours. While Rory whooped in excitement, Jake tried to catch the eye of the servant who'd looked at him earlier, but the men just bowed and left.

Jake and Rory sat on the end of their very large beds. Jake lay back. It was the softest mattress he had ever felt. He could have fallen asleep instantly.

'Can you believe this?' Rory said. 'I wish I lived like this all the time.'

They started looking around the room. Everything was carefully made. Jake thought it must have taken years to create. He ran his hand over a row of jewels that made musical notes as he touched them. He was making up a tune when there was a knock on the door. It swung open before he could answer it.

There stood Henry. Or at least he thought it was Henry. He'd had a complete makeover. He was dressed in bright yellow robes and wore a small bronze crown on his head. He spun around.

'What do you think?' he said, smiling.

Rory leaned in towards him, staring at his face. 'Have you had your eyebrows waxed?'

Henry's smile faded.

'Don't mind him, he's just jealous,' Jake said. 'You look fantastic.'

'There is more! Look what they gave me!' Henry exclaimed.

He opened up his arm. His control panel shone bronze like his crown and there were tiny sapphires, rubies and even diamonds inside.

'Wow!' Jake said. 'I guess that means you don't think our hosts are pirates anymore?'

'Of course not,' Henry said. 'Pirates steal from others. They do not give a person gifts.'

Jake wondered at the change in Henry. It seemed he was easily won over. But he felt relieved because if Henry didn't think they were pirates, they could all go back to enjoying themselves.

'Rory,' he said, 'you know the servants?'

'*Helpers*, you mean,' he said.

'Yeah, them,' Jake replied. 'Did any of them look worried to you?'

Rory frowned. 'No, why?'

'It doesn't matter –'

'Ah, excuse me,' Henry interrupted. Jake turned to see him lying fully clothed on his bed.

'We must get some sleep now if you will please cease talking,' Henry said. 'We need to be fully rested for tomorrow.' He placed a silk eye mask over his face and shut himself down.

35

'I guess he has a point,' Rory said and lay down on his bed too.

He started snoring the moment his head hit the pillow. Jake lay down too, but even though he was in the softest of soft beds he couldn't fall asleep. *Maybe I'm just overexcited,* he thought.

He tossed and turned until finally he gave up trying to sleep. His mum always went for walks in the night when she couldn't sleep. He decided to do the same and see if that would help.

This time the doors weren't locked and Jake stepped quietly into the golden hallway. It was empty, and glistened so brightly it hurt his eyes. As he walked, he wondered what it would be like to live like this all the time, with people serving you meals and with everything you could ever need or want. He suddenly felt homesick, even worse than when he'd landed at Remedial Space Car Driving School for a week. There was something unhomely about the megaship. Maybe it was all the shiny surfaces. Or maybe it was just because it didn't feel like anyone else even lived here. Even though it was fun staying for a night, he thought he would probably get bored of it pretty quickly.

There were several doors off the hallway that looked like the one he had come out of. He looked inside the rooms. They were like dormitories, with bunks to fit eight people in each room. They were plain, though – nothing like the luxurious room he was staying in. And they were mysteriously empty. The beds were neatly made with a sheet and grey blanket at the end of each one but there were no bags or belongings of any kind.

Jake walked past more closed doors until he saw one that made him stop. This one was very plain and there were no door handles. Instead this looked like a sliding door. He pressed his hand on it. It was cold to the touch. He gently pushed the door and to his surprise it slid open.

Jake gasped when he entered the room. It was like stepping inside a giant treasure chest. The room was piled high with all the gold and silver he could imagine, and dazzling gems of all colours and sizes. It was like pieces of a rainbow had been chopped up and thrown on top of the pot of gold at the end of it.

He stepped around the room, careful not to knock any of the treasure. There was only enough room for him to edge around with his back pressed against the wall. *Wait until the others hear about this!* Jake thought. They wouldn't believe it. He'd never seen so many riches in his life.

On one side of the treasure pile he saw a shiny nugget of gold poking out. It looked enormous, but it was wedged in a pile of silver.

He pulled on the nugget. It hardly moved. He pulled harder.

The nugget came loose in his hands and Jake gasped at the size of it. Then a soft clinking noise came from the pile and Jake looked up. *Uh-oh.* A piece of silver dropped into the place where the nugget had been. Then another dropped, and another, and then the whole pile began to collapse, clanging and falling like dominos.

Realising Violet and the others were likely to hear the noise, Jake ran for the door. He bolted down the hallway and slipped into his room just as Em appeared from around the far corner.

Jake leaped into bed and pulled up the covers, his heart racing. *Phew*, he thought. *That was close!*

Jake woke his friends early the next morning

and gathered them together. He sat on the edge of his bed and described what he'd seen. By the end of it they were all staring at him like he'd just told them he was really an alien.

'Are you sure you weren't just dreaming?' Rory said sleepily.

'Sometimes it feels like my dreams are real,' Milly added.

'That is the most likely explanation,' Henry agreed.

Only Skye seemed to take Jake's story seriously.

'Why would they be keeping all that treasure?' she asked.

'That's just it – I don't know,' Jake mused. 'Henry, I think you were onto something. What if they really *are* pirates?'

Henry fiddled with the panel in his arm and said nothing.

'Jake's right. They have to be pirates. The

treasure must have been stolen. Where else could all the precious metals and stones have come from?' Skye agreed.

'And have you noticed the only people here are Violet, Ruby, Em and Indigo?' Jake said. 'Plus a few servants.'

'Helpers,' Rory corrected.

'And they didn't know we were coming, or that we were on a mystery flight. Don't you see? They really are pirates!' Jake insisted.

Jake expected Henry to be the first to snap into action. But instead he closed over the panel in his arm and sat with his hands folded on his lap.

'Come on! We've got to sneak out of here before they wake up!'

'No, I was wrong. I do not believe they are pirates after all,' Henry said, shaking his crown like he was king.

'What?' Jake asked, confused.

'There is clearly a logical explanation for this.'

Jake couldn't believe what Henry was saying. 'But you were the one who said they were pirates in the first place,' he reminded Henry.

Henry frowned and pushed his crown back on his head. Jake realised Henry must have been sucked in by the pirates when they gave him the fancy clothes and a control panel makeover. He had been easily won over all right. Henry could stay but Jake decided he was going to get out, and everyone else agreed they should escape.

'We're leaving now, Henry,' he announced. 'You can come with us or stay here forever as their servant.'

But when Jake wrenched open the door he found Violet, Ruby, Indigo and Em standing in front of it.

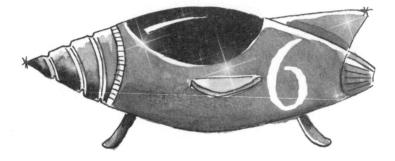

Jake gulped.

'Going somewhere?' Violet said smoothly.

'Oh, ah, no,' Jake said, 'we were just, ah –'

'– so excited we couldn't sleep,' Skye added.

Jake liked her quick thinking. She always seemed to come up with something good when things got scary.

'Hmmm, I see,' Violet said, smiling. 'Em thought he heard a little noise coming from

44

our treasure room last night.'

Em nodded and Jake looked at the floor, hoping he wouldn't give himself away.

'You are probably wondering what we are doing with all that treasure?' Violet continued.

Jake didn't look up.

'I guess we should have explained earlier. Ruby?'

'We are the Treasure Guards,' Ruby explained. 'We travel around the solar system and make sure people's most precious things are kept safe.'

'You mean you steal people's things?' Rory said.

Skye, Milly and Jake all glared at him and he frowned, realising he'd just given them away.

'How about an early breakfast, then we'll take you on a special trip to show you around Saturn? You can see exactly what we do then,' Violet said sweetly.

45

'I don't know –' Jake began.

'It's all part of the mystery flight,' Violet said. 'I'm sure your friend Henry will tell you that we are very generous people too.'

Jake turned to Henry, who was standing behind them. He was smiling and nodding as though in a trance. It didn't look like he was going to be much help at all. The four agreed to go.

Jake and his friends followed the four 'Treasure Guards' down the long hallway to the dining room. *Treasure Guards?* Jake thought. *More like Treasure Thieves.*

At the table, the servants delivered them all a delicious-looking breakfast. Violet and her friends left them to eat. Jake looked closely at the servant who had looked like he wanted to tell him something. This time he kept his head lowered, like the others, and didn't utter a word. They finished serving and disappeared through the doors again.

Jake thought he might need his energy for whatever lay ahead so decided to have some breakfast. He had no choice but to go along with things for now. If Violet and her crew really were pirates they weren't going to let them just fly out of here anyway.

He picked up his napkin. As he unfolded it a small note fell out. Making sure no-one was looking, Jake opened the piece of paper.

Something was scribbled on it. It said:

We have been captured. Help us!

Captured? So these were not kind, peaceful people – they really *were* pirates! Jake looked at his friends. Would they even believe the note was real? He'd have to find a way to explain – but not while Henry was around.

Jake wondered how they could help. If they could get to the Galactic Explorer 5000

they could fly out and alert the CIA, but that seemed impossible right now. They hadn't even been able to escape the dining room last night. Jake quickly folded the piece of paper and stuffed it in his pocket. One thing was certain. They were on another mission after all.

After breakfast, the pirates led them back down the hallway for their 'tour of Saturn'. Jake knew that was a lie, but he had no idea what the pirates would do with them instead. And he had to tell Skye, Milly and Rory what was going on – but how? Jake wondered if the CIA had programmed the mystery flight. If they had, did they mean to send them to the pirates' megaship or just to Saturn? Did they even know the planet's megaship had been taken over by pirates? Henry would know the answers, but Jake was pretty sure they couldn't trust him now. From the way he was chatting with the pirates, it seemed likely that he'd lock Jake up himself.

As they walked Jake tried to think of a way to escape. But before he knew it they were inside the gold-lined hangar again, and next to the Galactic Explorer 5000 was a sleek, glittering space car. Like everything else on the megaship it was made of precious metal. The front of it was spiral-shaped, like a drill, and the whole thing was narrow and streamlined.

Jake wished they could just make a dash for the Explorer and get out of here. But he knew the pirates would be able to overpower them. Even if they did make it to the car he didn't know how to take the car out of autopilot, or even how to open the trapdoor at the top of the hangar.

Violet led them to the narrow space car and they all climbed inside. Everything gleamed with gold and jewels. They were about to travel first-class. If Jake hadn't been so scared about what would become of them he would have been super excited.

While the pirates were busy preparing for take-off, Jake sneakily passed the note around so the others could read it. He knew not to let Henry see it, though. But Henry was too busy learning about the special craft they were on, saying 'Ooh!' and 'Aaah!' every time the pirates showed him something. Rory nodded towards Henry and rolled his eyes at Jake. Then he read the note and suddenly looked paler than the moonstones studded on the space car's chairs. They all sat back, stunned. Jake wondered again where they were going. What exactly would the crew of pirates do with them if they became their new prisoners?

They flew out into space until the megaship looked tiny, like just another star in the solar system. The car made its way around Saturn and Jake had no idea where they were headed until he saw something appear on the projection screen in front of Em, who was driving. It was one of the moons of Saturn and they were heading straight towards it.

'Er, excuse me,' Jake asked. 'Why are we

going to a moon?'

Violet turned to them and smiled. But now her smile didn't look so calm and friendly. This was more of an evil grin.

'You did agree you'd like to find out exactly what we do?' Violet said.

'Yes,' Jake mumbled.

'Well, the moon we are heading towards is Titan,' Violet said. 'You could say that *we guard* its treasure.' Jake heard Em and Indigo snigger quietly in the front.

Titan? Jake had learned about this moon at school. No-one on Earth knew what was beneath its thick atmosphere but he guessed they were about to find out. He gulped nervously.

'Now, make sure you are securely strapped into your seats,' Violet commanded. 'This is going to be a fast and bumpy ride.'

Jake looked at his friends. Milly had her

head pressed hard against the back of her seat already. Rory looked like he was about to explode from holding his breath. Skye was strapping herself in so tight she looked like she was about to be split in half. The space car quickly gathered speed, wobbling from side to side with the force.

Soon they reached the atmosphere of Titan. It was thick and cloudy. Jake gazed out the front screen of the car. He couldn't see anything. It was like being in an orange fog. But as they moved in further the space around the car cleared and Jake saw what looked like a giant glass dome over the surface of the moon. It was made of triangular segments of thick glass, and they were fast approaching it.

Ruby pulled out a remote and pressed it. A large triangular segment opened up and the car passed through it. They were now inside the dome and the car was surrounded by a golden haze. As they came closer to the surface Jake could see that Titan looked a lot like Earth, only it shone as though it was completely made of gold.

Jake, Milly and Skye all looked at each other. Rory stared blankly as though he was a frozen ice particle. The air around the car was filled with tiny particles of dust as well as gold and silver glitter. The sparkles looked magical as they rose and fell, but Jake was filled with dread.

Everyone was silent as the space car came in to land on Titan's surface. It still looked like Earth, except here huge slabs of the ground had been cut out and the land seemed bare and lifeless – all dust and dirt and big gaping holes.

As they got closer to the surface Jake could see they were heading towards a mine site. There were huge diggers and cranes everywhere. People wearing overalls and safety helmets were running around and driving the equipment. The space car slid along a landing strip as Em stopped the car.

'What is this place?' Milly gasped.

'We found this moon quite by accident while exploring around Saturn,' Violet explained. 'It was very lucky we found it when there are so many moons around. It doesn't look like much from the surface but underneath it's the biggest treasure chest you have ever seen.'

'You're mining this place for treasure?' Skye asked, her eyes wide.

Violet nodded, actually looking proud of herself. 'We don't need to travel around the solar system stealing treasure anymore. It's all right here, waiting for us.'

'I knew it! You *are* pirates!' Rory said angrily.

'But of course,' Violet replied. 'We couldn't let you know that until we were safely away from the megaship though.'

'That's right,' Ruby added. 'We had to wait until Henry was completely under our control, and we had to be sure there was no chance of you escaping from us on the Explorer.'

'But … where did all these workers come from?' Jake asked, with a sinking feeling in his stomach.

'They're the people of Saturn,' Ruby explained. 'An extra bonus was that Titan is very Earth-like so it was easy to put them straight to work here. Once the dome was built, of course.'

'And now we have four new workers to join our crew,' Violet said. 'It was lucky that your mystery flight accidentally brought you to us. You'll come in very handy. Especially with a cyborg to help.'

Her sweet smile had been completely replaced with that dark scowl Jake had glimpsed earlier.

'Welcome to your new home,' Ruby laughed.

Jake, Rory, Skye and Milly were marched out of the space car and led across the tarmac towards the mining site. Henry followed behind them, talking with Em and Indigo like they were old friends.

Jake shuddered. They were now under the pirates' control. Once they were left here as miners there would be no way of getting off this moon. And what about the people of Saturn? There had to be a way of saving them, but Henry sure wasn't going to be any help. Jake couldn't believe how easily he had turned to the pirates' side, especially when Jake and his friends were being sent to the mines as slaves – maybe for the rest of their lives.

The more he thought about it the angrier he got. He knew Henry was a little different but he'd thought they were friends. Jake trudged along unhappily, not even caring what hard work might lie ahead of them.

'Here we are,' Violet said, stopping them at the mine site. 'Em will give you a uniform and safety gear. Then he'll leave you with your supervisor. Oh, and we'll stay awhile to make sure you start work properly.' She pointed to a tall, narrow tower on top of a hill above the mine, then floated off towards it with Ruby and Indigo following behind.

Skye turned to Em. 'You won't get away with this,' she snapped.

'Really?' Em laughed. 'I think we've been getting away with it pretty well so far. We have all the slaves we could need and they all do as we say because they can't get off Titan unless we collect them.'

Jake could see that the pirates had the perfect plan. There was no way of escape, and no way of letting anyone know where they were. No-one could escape a moon without a space car.

They followed Em to a small room where they were all fitted with uniforms, helmets and heavy boots. Henry was given a uniform too. It looked the same as theirs but his had a darker coloured jacket. Jake wondered what Henry thought of his new pirate friends now that he was going to be left here as well.

When they were all dressed, Em led them out to the work site. Jake stared down at a gaping hole. Inside he could see a shiny thread of gold running through the creamy-coloured rock.

'You will be working in the gold mines,' Em said. 'I'll leave you with your supervisor now.'

Jake frowned and looked around but there was no-one else there.

'I can't see our supervisor,' Jake said.

'He's right here,' he said, pointing at Henry. 'Say hello to your new boss.'

Em chuckled as Jake and his friends stared, shocked, at the cyborg. Henry gave them a half-smile and waved. He seemed almost apologetic and laughed nervously.

'Are you kidding?' Rory screamed. 'I'm not taking orders from him!'

'Suit yourself,' Em said, 'but you either do as Henry says or be cast off the planet. We might be different to the pirates you've heard about but we still know all about walking the plank – the plank into space.'

Em laughed loudly at his own joke. No-one else did – not even Henry.

'We have inserted an excellent planning program into your cyborg friend,' Em explained, still cackling noisily. 'This is going to be our best treasure haul yet!'

When Em had marched back towards the observation tower to join Violet and the others, Rory was the first to turn on Henry.

'You traitor!' he yelled.

'It's not his fault, Rory,' Skye argued. 'Those horrible pirates have implanted that program into him.'

'I always knew a cyborg couldn't be trusted,' Rory growled back, staring at Henry. 'And I was right.'

'Whatever they've done, we're not going to figure out a way out of here by fighting,' Milly said.

'There *is* no way out of here. You heard them,' Rory cried.

'There's always a way out,' Jake whispered so Henry couldn't hear, 'but for now we'd better just do as they say and follow Henry's orders. I don't want to walk the plank into space.' Jake pointed to the observation tower.

'He's right,' Skye said.

'Attention!' Henry snapped. 'It is time to work!'

At the mine site, Jake picked at the rock for hours until his arms ached and sweat poured down his face. He racked his brain for an escape plan but it was hard to think when he was so tired. Every now and then he glanced up at the tower. He couldn't see the pirates because they were so high up, but he could imagine them smiling and laughing as their slaves pulled treasure from the ground.

Henry had shown them how to follow

63

the gold threads in the rock and extract the precious metal from the earth. He sure knew a lot for someone who'd probably never even seen a mine before. It was amazing what a computer program could do.

Before long they had a cart filled to the brim with shining pieces of gold rock. The four of them hauled the cart up to the surface and pulled it along the rocky ground towards the tower. *What an amazing moon this is,* Jake thought tiredly, but he felt sad that it was being pulled apart to make a few people rich.

'This must have been a beautiful place before the pirates found it,' Skye said, as if she had heard his thoughts.

And now there was no way to escape it.

As they moved their cart towards the tower a bell sounded around the work site. All the miners stopped work and headed towards a large shed-like building.

'Where do you think they're going?' Milly asked.

'I'd say it's the end of the work day,' Rory said, looking at his watch.

'Do you think everyone lives in there?' Milly said, pointing at the shed.

'They must,' Skye replied. 'I wonder what we do now? Henry?'

But Henry just shrugged. Obviously that information wasn't part of his program. As they were deciding whether to leave the cart and head over with everyone else Violet appeared, having come down from her tower. She looked inside the cart.

'Not too bad for a first day,' she said, rubbing her hands together. 'Load it up into the car and then you will be finished for the day.' She pointed at the same car they had arrived in.

The friends stared at her silently, not moving.

'You will learn to do as we say or you will have no chance of ever returning home,' she said, smiling.

When they got to the car, Jake was the first to start loading the gold into the back of it. He doubted anyone ever got to go home once they were here, but until they could think of a plan they just had to do what they were told. He remembered the servant's note. How was he meant to help him – or anyone else, for that matter? With Henry reprogrammed and no way of leaving, it looked like this was the first CIA mission they were going to fail.

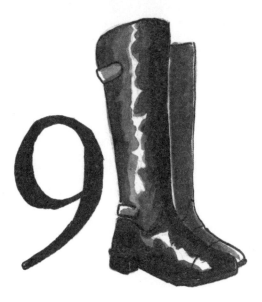

After they had finished loading up the space car with gold, Em told them that the four pirates were leaving Titan and returning to the megaship for one week. He left instructions for Henry and then followed the other pirates into the treasure-filled space car. Jake watched helplessly as it sped down the runway and disappeared.

'What do we do now?' asked Milly in a shaky voice.

Skye put her arm around Milly. 'We follow everyone else until we figure out what to do,' she said, trying to smile.

The four of them headed towards the big shed, ignoring Henry who followed behind. When they arrived, workers were still piling in and there was a big queue out the door. They joined the end of it, not even knowing what the queue was for. Jake decided to ask the person in front of them in the line.

'Excuse me,' said Jake as he tapped the man on the shoulder.

The man turned around. He looked sad and Jake felt sorry for him. Jake realised the man was trapped on Titan, just like him – maybe forever.

'Sorry,' Jake said, 'but we're new here –'

'I can see that,' the man said. 'Nice pressed uniforms and shiny boots and all.' He half-smiled at Jake. 'I'm Paul. I guess you want to know how things work around here?'

Jake nodded. They introduced themselves and huddled in to listen.

'This here's the dormitory. It's where we eat, sleep and shower,' Paul explained, pointing at the shed. 'The queue is for dinner. First things first.' He winked.

Jake was glad someone was being nice to them. He didn't feel they were so alone on this strange planet now.

'How long have you been here?' Skye asked.

'Oh, it's hard to keep track of time,' he said. 'But I'd say about five years.'

'Five years!' Milly exclaimed.

'I know it's hard to imagine living so long in such a place,' Paul added as the line of workers moved slowly forward, 'but you get kind of used to it. I do miss my old home on the megaship though. It was a simple but wonderful place to live before the pirates took it over.'

'Where did they come from?' Rory questioned.

'Nowhere as far as I can tell,' Paul answered. 'They've always travelled around the solar system, stealing whatever they could.'

'If they're already thieves, why do they need to mine Titan for more treasure?' Skye asked, frowning.

'The pirates say they want to settle down somewhere and not have to chase people for jewels anymore,' Paul explained. 'When they found what was on Titan they laughed and said they'd never have to work for treasure again.'

'So they're lazy as well as greedy?' Jake said, grimacing.

They had reached the food counter. Paul leaned over and grabbed a bowl, filling it with a thick soup as green as the grass back on Earth. Jake frowned at Paul's muck.

'Good luck kids,' he said.

Paul moved away to one of the tables. Most were already filled with workers who were slurping on soup and talking tiredly to each other.

'Come on, hurry it up!' someone yelled from further back in the queue.

Jake quickly filled his bowl. Not everyone here was as friendly as Paul.

After dinner Jake and his friends moved to the dormitory. There were single beds lined up in rows. After walking up and down the aisles for a while, they found four empty beds on the far side of the room. Rory picked one and threw his boots under it. The girls placed their boots neatly at the end of theirs. Skye folded the top of her blanket down in a triangle. Jake slumped down on the end of his, the springs squeaking under his weight.

'There seem to be only four beds available here,' Henry said.

'That's right,' Rory said. 'And they're all taken.'

Henry frowned and slowly walked away. Jake almost felt sorry for him.

The next thing he knew, the lights were turned off.

'Wow, five years,' Milly whispered. 'I don't think I can stand another minute here.'

'There's got to be a way off this moon,' Skye said softly. 'We just have to work it out.'

Rory snorted. 'I can't see any way out. If all these adults haven't been able to figure it out, how are *we* supposed to?'

'I don't know,' Jake admitted.

'We don't even have Henry's cyborg skills now he's working for the pirates,' Skye added.

'I think we just need a good sleep and we'll be able to think better in the morning,' Jake suggested.

'He's right,' Milly said.

'Shhh!' someone whispered at them.

Jake didn't know if sleep would really help, but there was nothing more they could say tonight. He pulled up his thin blanket and tried to sleep.

Sometime during the night Jake felt a tap on his shoulder. He rolled over and tried to go back to sleep but whoever it was tapped harder, then nudged him awake. His eyes flicked open. In the dimness he could just make out the shape of Henry. He didn't know why the cyborg was trying to wake him up but he didn't want to see him right now. He knew he'd need his sleep if he was going to be digging up rock all the next day. His first few hours in the mine had been tiring enough.

'Go away,' he whispered.

But Henry wasn't going anywhere. This

time he grabbed Jake's blanket and pulled it right off him. When Jake tried to pull it back up, he couldn't. Henry had a firm hold of it.

'Get up!' Henry hissed. 'And be quiet.'

Jake had no choice but to follow him. They crept to the bathroom at one end of the dormitory. Henry closed the door and turned on the sink, letting the water run.

'What are you doing? Jake said sleepily. 'Some of us have to work tomorrow.'

'Listen! We have to be quick. The pirates think they have reprogrammed me but the CIA inserted a backup program that overrides anything else attached to my control panel. After the Robot Games they wanted to be sure that no-one but the CIA could change my program.'

'So you're not really on the pirates' side?' Jake asked, unsure whether to believe him.

'No, of course not. Cyborgs do not care for

fancy clothes and jewels,' Henry said. 'But I had to let them think they had reprogrammed me or they would guess.'

'Guess what?' Jake asked.

'That I am a CIA agent. The minute I saw the megaship and it overrode our system I knew it was pirates who had taken it over.'

'But we didn't listen to you, and now we're trapped here,' Jake said. Everything made sense now. 'Why didn't you tell us earlier? We could have tried to escape before we left the megaship!'

'The pirates have attached a bug to me,' Henry explained.

'Eww, no wonder you don't like the pirates after all,' Jake said, surprised. 'I would too if someone squished a space bug on me.'

'Not a space bug! A bug – a listening device,' Henry said quickly. 'They can hear everything that is said. But I found it. And I can turn it off and on. However I cannot leave it off for long or they will guess something is wrong.'

'What are we going to do?' Jake asked.

'We have to get everyone off Titan,' Henry said. 'That is the mission.'

'That's really helpful Henry,' Jake groaned. 'Can't you contact the CIA? They could rescue everyone in a day.'

'I cannot. The glass in this dome is too thick. The distress signal will not make it through,' Henry explained. 'We need to complete the mission ourselves.'

'And how exactly are we going to do that?'

'I am sure you will come up with something,' Henry smiled.

Jake and his friends worked hard in the mines like all the other workers. But all the time Jake was trying to come up with a plan to free everyone from Titan. As hard as he tried he just couldn't think of anything. Without a space car there was just no way they could get off the moon.

Before breakfast that morning, Jake had quickly explained to everyone how Henry was faking being reprogrammed and how he was on their side. Skye and Milly were relieved. Even Rory had to admit that he'd been wrong about Henry.

During the day Henry kept up his act, snapping instructions at them from the top of the mine. But he also walked away from the pit a few times to allow them time to talk secretly without his bug picking up their conversation and sending it straight back to the pirates.

At the end of their long and tiring day, the four of them sat around the table for dinner. Jake pushed his food around his plate with his fork. Even though he was hungry after all that hard work, he didn't feel like eating. Not even Skye could come up with any plans for escape.

'It's not fair,' Rory complained. 'The pirates are enjoying themselves back on the megaship while we're stuck here working and eating sludge.'

'Those pirates are so greedy,' Milly huffed.

'They could never use all that treasure they already have and they're still taking more,' Skye agreed.

Jake looked up from his plate. 'Say that last part again, Skye,' he said.

'They're still taking more?' Skye said, confused.

'That's it!' Jake cried, as loudly as he dared in the crowded dining hall. 'That's how we'll get off Titan.'

'What are you talking about?' Rory said, sitting up straight.

'They're greedy,' he said. 'We can use their greed.'

Jake stayed awake most of that night working out his plan. The others agreed it could work, but everything had to be ready by the time the pirates returned. There wasn't much time.

Henry climbed into the mine the next morning, pretending to inspect their digging work. He switched off his bug while Jake explained his idea.

'It is an excellent plan,' Henry nodded. 'Now you must convince the rest of the slaves to help you. We do not want anyone left behind.'

This was the hardest part, and at first it didn't work out very well. No-one on Titan believed the kids could free them from their life of slavery. They either laughed in their faces or told them to get back to work before they got in trouble with the pirates. Some workers tried to be kind, telling them there was no hope and that they just had to get on with life on Titan. Others were annoyed and thought they were just a bunch of silly kids who were stopping them from doing their work.

One evening, the friends sat by the edge of the mine, chewing on flavourless pieces of

80

bread. All the fresh food had run out until the pirates returned with more. They were worn out and frustrated. The other workers had stopped talking to them now and Jake felt very alone. He watched the fragments of gold and dust floating in the air. It was actually amazing to see. He just wished he wasn't trapped here. He thought of his mum and dad back home and felt worse than ever.

'Maybe we should just free ourselves and leave the workers here,' Rory suggested. 'The CIA will be able to work something out to get them later.'

'We can't do that!' Milly argued. 'It wouldn't be right.'

Skye spoke firmly. 'We have to get everyone out at once or we won't be able to trap the pirates here.' It was Jake who finally had an idea.

'We have to *show* everyone how the plan

will work. If they can see it for themselves, they'll believe us.'

'We'll never get everyone to stop work for that,' Rory said, shrugging.

'What about that worker we first met? Paul?' Skye suggested. 'If he sees what we're doing he might be able to convince the others to try it.'

'He was nice to us when we first arrived,' Milly said.

They all agreed. It was the best chance they had.

The pirates were due back in a few days' time, and Jake and his friends worked harder than ever on their plan. Using some of the gold they had already pulled from the ground, they planted a fake seam of gold within the rock in the mine. It ended in a half-buried blob of gold that looked like it disappeared far underground. When they showed Paul the fake gold seam on the day the pirates were due to return, he chuckled and clapped Jake on the back.

'This could really be our way off this moon. It's worth a try anyway. You leave the other workers to me,' he said with a grin, shaking Jake's hand before he left.

Barely a minute later Jake saw the pirates' space car enter the atmosphere, returning to collect their next haul of treasure. He took a deep breath. The next bit was up to Henry and his acting skills.

The moment the four pirates stepped out of their space car, Henry ran over to them.

'Violet! Violet!' he cried, waving his arms in the air.

'Yessss?' Violet said slowly, looking worried.

'I have some excellent news,' Henry said.

Violet's lips curled up into a smile. 'Go on,' she said.

'The crew I am in charge of has found the largest gold seam you have ever seen.'

'Really?' Violet said, her eyes narrowing.

'Come! I will show you.'

Henry turned to Jake and his friends, putting on a very bad-tempered face. 'Hurry up and show them where you found the gold,' he barked.

If Jake didn't know Henry was faking it he would have still believed he was on the pirates' side. The cyborg ordered them into line and led them towards the mine. The pirates followed behind. When Jake pointed out the fake seam of gold, the pirates' eyes widened with greed. Jake could almost see the gold reflected in their eyes.

'Very good,' Violet said. 'Henry, have your team get it out of the ground and you will be well rewarded when you return to the megaship.'

'I knew a cyborg would do better than an ordinary human worker,' Em said, rubbing his hands together.

'There is only one problem,' Henry said.

Violet's eyebrows knitted together in a frown. 'Yessss?'

'We'll need a bigger space craft to get it back to the megaship.'

Violet started laughing, the bell-like sound echoing through the mine.

'That is no problem at all. We'll use that enormous Galactic Explorer of yours. There's more than enough room for the gold in there.' Her smile faded as she turned to Jake and his friends. 'We will return in three days. Have the gold ready by then.'

'I have already given my instructions to my team,' Henry said.

'Yes, of course,' Violet sneered. 'For now, you will come back with us, Henry. We wouldn't trust just any of our workers with getting the Explorer ready for a treasure haul.'

Certainly,' Henry said. 'But you will need someone else to drive it back with me. It's so big it needs at least two drivers.'

'One of the servants will drive it back with you,' Violet said. 'This is going to be worth it, I know.'

Henry cackled along with the pirates as they walked off and climbed onto their space craft again. Jake was relieved they had managed to trick the pirates. Now they just had the last part of their plan to go.

They watched the pirates' car fly through the entry point in the dome, then walked back down to the mine site. The workers had stopped digging and were forming a crowd in the middle of the main pit. They were all staring at Jake, Skye, Milly and Rory. Jake had never felt so scared. He hoped they had

agreed to the plan.

When they got closer, they saw Paul standing at the front of the crowd. He started clapping. Then another worker joined in, and another until all the workers were cheering 'Freedom, freedom' and clapping. Jake looked to Skye. She was wiping away a tear. It looked like there was hope of them escaping this place and saving everyone after all.

Over the next few days everyone worked hard to collect carts and the dirt to put inside them. Meanwhile, Jake and his friends mined some real gold. Next, they drilled breathing holes in the bottom of the carts. On the third morning, when the pirates were due to return, the workers piled into the huge carts. Jake and his friends scooped some dirt over them and then covered the dirt with gold. It looked like the carts were full to the brim with the precious metal. They lined the carts up at the base of the pirates' tower.

When the pirates returned later that morning, Henry flew in close behind them in the new treasure craft. Violet's eyes glowed when she stepped out of her space car and saw the heaped carts.

'Well, you little people *have* been busy!' she said.

Jake and his friends stood by the carts. They'd covered their faces with dirt so it looked like they'd been busy mining the gold.

'But where are all the other workers?' Em asked, frowning.

'There … ah, there was so much gold they had to help us,' Jake stammered.

'Yes, they're having a break, in the big shed,' Skye added.

'Very well,' Violet said, still staring greedily at the gold. 'Load the carts onto the Explorer.'

Jake nodded and the four of them pushed the heavy carts into the car's new storage bay. Rory fell behind the others.

'Hurry it up,' Henry yelled. 'Come on Mr I-Know-Everything. Move faster.'

Rory scowled. Jake hid a smile.

Finally, they loaded the last cart into the back of the Explorer. The workers were safely hidden on board.

Jake walked around the car and approached Violet. 'All the carts are now loaded on,' Jake told her.

Everything was going to plan. There was just one thing left to do.

'Wait!' Henry said, running up behind Jake.

'What is it?' Violet snapped. Jake could see that she was so eager to take the gold back to the megaship that she couldn't think about anything else.

'There is another thing I wish to show you.

From the tower,' he said.

'What is it?'

'There is something else I located,' Henry said. 'I was not sure earlier, but my team has just confirmed it. There is more treasure. But it is on the other side of the mine site so you have to be up high to see it.'

Violet scowled. 'This had better be good,' she grumbled, following after Henry. Ruby, Indigo and Em didn't look convinced.

'It is even better than gold!' Henry added.

That caught their attention and they eagerly followed Henry up the tower.

As soon as the pirates entered the tower, Jake, Skye, Milly and Rory sped over to the Galactic Explorer and climbed in the hatch. They were surprised when they saw who was sitting in the driver's seat.

'What ...?' Rory stammered, as Jake looked

over the back of the seat. It was the servant who had handed Jake the note back at the megaship. This time his head wasn't bowed down but was lifted proudly.

'Hello!' he said, standing up. 'Henry told the pirates he needed an ace pilot to drive the Galactic Explorer out of here. I'm Spitfire, by the way.'

'Spitfire?' Rory said.

'It's my racing name,' Spitfire replied. 'I went off-course in the Ace Space Race a few years back and flew straight into Violet's megaship. I might have been trapped here. Now's my chance to show them all,' he hooted.

'Sounds good to me,' Jake said, smiling. 'Once you drive the pirates' car away from Titan they'll have no way of escaping – they'll be trapped here forever!'

The five of them quickly helped the workers out from inside the carts, digging out the dirt and pieces of gold. They came out one by one, looking like some kind of rock creatures as they shook dirt and flakes of gold from their clothes. Jake laughed. Through their dirty faces he could see their white teeth as they smiled. Their eyes shone brightly from behind dusty eyelashes. Jake had never felt as good about something he'd achieved as he did right now.

All they had to do now was wait for Henry to return. Jake could hear his heart thumping in his chest like a drum. If the last part of the plan didn't work they would all be caught and would be forced to walk the plank into space, lost forever.

Finally, after what seemed like hours, Henry appeared through the hatch. 'Ready?' he said.

'Did you lock them inside?' Jake asked.

'Yes, while they were busy trying to see where the treasure was I ran out of the tower.

Those silly pirates still believed I was on their side until I slammed the door closed and they discovered I had locked them in the tower,' he said.

The plan had worked. It was time to get off Titan for good and leave the pirates trapped there forever.

'I'm ready to get set for take-off,' said Spitfire. 'Eat my space dust, pirates!' He leaped out of the hatch and darted off to the pirates' space car.

Skye took up the rear navigation seat in the Galactic Explorer.

'I guess you figured out how to override the auto-pilot?' she said to Henry.

'Of course. It was not hard to do after all,' Henry replied, grinning.

She brought up the projection screen, zooming in on the pirates' car behind them. Milly took charge of the controls and Rory sat in the pilot seat. Henry sat in the co-pilot seat, ready to activate the remote to open the entry point in the dome. Jake buckled himself in the front projection position, his hands shaking like the pool of jelly they'd sat in at the Floating Hotel of Venus. It slowed him down as he tried to do up the clips. Finally, they were all done and ready to go.

'Start the engines, Milly,' Jake said.

She switched the car on and Rory prepared for take-off. Jake turned to the workers who were crowded into the storage bay.

'Ready to leave this place?' he said.

The people of Saturn cheered.

Rory shifted into drive. 'Then let's go!' he cried.

They were just lifting off when Skye yelled out a warning.

'What is it?' Jake cried.

'It's the pirates!' she exclaimed, staring at

the rear projection screen.

Jake didn't need to see Skye's face to know that things had gone wrong. *Really* wrong. He twisted around to see the rear screen. The pirates had somehow broken out of the tower and were racing towards the space car that Spitfire was driving. The car started moving forward but not fast enough. The pirates leaped on board.

'Stop the car. We have to go back!' Skye cried.

'No!' Henry said. 'The pirates will catch us if we do that. Our only chance is to beat them to the dome and close it before they can reach it.'

'But the pirates will just open it again with their remote,' Rory argued.

'I had already computed that possibility,' Henry said. He reached down and pulled out a second remote, grinning. 'I took this from

96

their car in case things went wrong. They cannot open the dome without it.'

'You've forgotten one thing,' Jake said.

'I do not think so,' Henry said.

'Spitfire!' the four friends said together.

Henry's smile disappeared. 'Oh! It appears you are right. I had not thought of that.'

Skye gasped. 'They've thrown him from the car!'

They saw Spitfire roll along the dusty ground. The pirates' car picked up speed and started heading towards the dome.

'We can't leave him there,' Milly said firmly.

Jake turned and looked at the workers. They were nodding. No-one wanted to leave a friend behind.

'You're right,' Jake agreed. 'Turn the car around, Rory. We have to try to save him, no matter what.'

R ory spun the car around in an expert move that even made Henry nod in approval. Jake worried they would never escape the pirates now but he knew they had to save Spitfire. He navigated for Rory as he came in close to where Spitfire had been thrown from the car.

'Oh no! The pirates have turned back around,' Skye cried. 'They're following us.'

'They must have realised Henry took the

remote,' Jake said.

'Yes, and they know that they cannot escape the dome without it,' Henry added.

'You mean they're after us?' Milly cried.

'Exactly!'

'And they're gaining on our car,' Skye yelled. 'Hurry, Rory!'

They skidded along the surface and stopped, collecting a shaken and dirty Spitfire.

'You should have left me behind and gone after Violet and her cronies,' Spitfire panted as Jake pulled him into the car. 'But since you didn't you'd better let me try to get us away from those pirates.' Rory quickly moved aside as Spitfire skidded over and took the driver's seat. 'Nice move back there, by the way,' he said to Rory, who looked pleased.

Jake wasn't sure that anyone could escape the pirates now, but Spitfire amazed them with his skills. It wasn't just his ace flying ability. He was able to get them all working together better than they ever had before. With just a few words he had Milly moving them at maximum speed, Jake navigating the shortest path to the dome's entry point and Rory helping control the car from the co-pilot's seat. Henry had the remote ready to use and Skye kept an eye out for anything behind them. But even with Spitfire driving the pirates were still close behind.

'The pirates are only seconds away from us,' Skye yelled. 'If we don't get some extra speed they'll make it through the dome before we have time to close it behind us.'

'We have to move faster, Milly,' Spitfire ordered.

Milly nodded and set the boosters for full speed.

'That's given us a bit more space,' Skye said, smiling, 'We'll still have to be fast though.'

'Henry, open the dome in twenty seconds.'

Henry nodded. Rory veered expertly until they were right in front of the opening. Henry pointed the remote towards it.

'Here we go!' Spitfire announced. 'Hang on tight.'

Jake felt the car moving so fast it was like they were a swurpie sucked up through a straw. Even Spitfire was sweating as he accelerated towards the dome.

'I'm going to need you all to help,' he yelled.

Skye and Jake snapped into action, watching their projection screens intently for the pirates' car while Jake called out positions to give them the best chance of getting through the entry point quickly. Milly monitored the car's speed control and Rory added extra steering to help Spitfire propel them in the right direction. Henry was concentrating on the dome and held the remote ready in his hand.

'We're almost there. Ready Henry?' Jake asked.

Henry nodded.

'When I give the signal, open up the dome,' Jake said.

'You'd better hurry,' Skye said. 'The pirates have hit their boosters and are right on our tail again. They're going to try to sneak through behind us.'

Jake glanced quickly at the workers. They were grouped in a corner looking scared. Paul, sitting at the front, was biting his nails. Another was fidgeting. Some were sitting so still they looked like they were lumps of rocks themselves. Jake half-smiled to reassure them. He looked at the screen again. The pirates were even closer now.

'We're never going to make it,' Rory cried.

'How much time do we have until they catch up?' Spitfire called.

'About ten seconds,' Skye yelped. 'Nine, eight ...'

'We're there. Open the entry,' Jake cried.

Henry pressed the button. The dome's entry point opened.

'Four ...' Skye counted.

The space car shot through the opening.

'Two ... and *close it!*' Skye yelled.

Henry pressed the button. The entry hatch swung back and snapped shut. The pirates' car swerved to miss the dome and disappeared down towards the surface of Titan.

'It worked!' Skye cried.

'We did it!' Jake screamed. 'We actually did it!'

They flew back towards the megaship, free at last. The people of Saturn piled out of the Galactic Explorer, thanking the team over and over again on their way out. Paul was the last to leave. He walked up to Jake.

'I don't know how to thank you,' he stammered.

'We're just glad you all agreed to go along with our plan,' he smiled. He watched Paul follow the others, catching up to his friends and wrapping his arms around their shoulders.

When Jake and his friends finally climbed out of the Explorer, the hangar seemed deserted. Then they saw two people standing at the far end near the huge crystal doors, waiting. It was Bree and Will, the CIA agents. Jake and his friends raced up to them.

'Good work team!' Bree said. 'We knew you could save the people of Saturn.'

'We couldn't have done it without Spitfire,' Jake said. 'He's the one who got us through that dome.'

Spitfire grinned, almost shyly. 'Thanks, kid,' he said. 'I'd have you lot as my crew anytime.'

'What's going to happen to the pirates?' Milly asked.

'I think they'll be very happy spending their days on a moon laden with treasure,' Will said. 'Wouldn't you agree?'

The others all laughed.

'So what about all the treasure on the megaship?' Rory asked.

Will scratched his chin. 'I think we could put it to better use than those greedy pirates did, that's for sure. But first, we have something special for you,' he said. 'Bree, would you do the honours?'

Jake wondered what it could be. Another secret mission? He watched with curiosity as Bree reached into her case and pulled out four badges. She leaned over and pinned one on Jake's grubby mining uniform. She then did the same to Skye, Milly and Rory. Jake read the badge upside-down: *Trainee CIA Agent.*

Wow! That sounded pretty awesome.

'Thanks!' he said.

'You're welcome,' Bree said. 'It's not every day a moon full of kidnapped people are rescued.'

'The first CIA training session is in one week's time,' Will added.

'Really?' Jake said. 'We're going to get *real* CIA training?'

'Yes, real training,' Bree laughed. 'We think you are ready for it.'

'Thank you so much!' Milly said.

'Will we get to use space cuffs?' Rory asked.

'Rory!' Skye exclaimed. 'Is there any pre-training reading we need to do?'

'No,' Will grinned. 'Just rest up, eat well and Henry will be back to take you to Headquarters in one week.'

'And no more mucking around wearing crowns and jewels now you're a – let me see –

a *senior agent*,' Bree smiled, reading from another badge. She pinned it onto Henry's shirt. Jake had never seen Henry grin so widely. Even Rory smiled and patted Henry on the back.

'Okay, you'd better take them home, Henry,' Will said.

'Maybe we shouldn't use the auto-pilot this time, Henry,' Jake said.

'Ah yes, Henry can explain that one to you all on the way home,' Will muttered.

'You set the course for Saturn!' Rory yelled.

'That is correct,' Henry said.

Rory went to grab Henry's arm but the cyborg interrupted. 'I did not know the megaship had been overtaken by pirates though,' he said quickly.

'Come on, let's go home,' Milly said. Rory huffed and followed the others to the Galactic Explorer 5000.

As they boarded, the people of Saturn came streaming back through the door of the hangar to say goodbye. It was the best feeling to see everyone looking happy. They waved as the five friends climbed inside and took up their positions.

Jake closed the hatch and switched on his screen, ready to head home. He looked at his CIA badge and smiled. He didn't know what lay ahead of them at the CIA but he couldn't wait to find out.

ABOUT THE AUTHOR

Candice enjoys writing stories about turbo space cars, hurtling asteroids and evil villains. Her quirky style, fast-paced narratives and originality appeal to reluctant boy readers in particular.

Following several years working in the media, Candice now devotes her time to her writing and to raising her two daughters.